I am Tasneem. Born and raised in the UAE, now I am a resident of this wonderful country. I am a Certified Human Resources Professional, a Motivation Counsellor, and a community worker.

This book will be my first write-up, and I will be writing more books in coming years, and would love to be known as a successful author.

In need of your love, support and prayers for me.

Thanks

# Tasneem Khamkar

## AMELIA

AUSTIN MACAULEY PUBLISHERS®

LONDON • CAMBRIDGE • NEW YORK • SHARJAH

ISBN – 9789948731948 – (Paperback)
ISBN – 9789948731955 – (E-Book)

Application Number: MC-10-01-8375569
Age Classification: E

The age group that matches the content of the books has been classified according to the age classification system issued by the UAE Media Council.

First Published 2024
AUSTIN MACAULEY PUBLISHERS FZE
Sharjah Publishing City
P.O Box [519201]
Sharjah, UAE
www.austinmacauley.ae
+971 655 95 202

Amelia, a girl who was from a poor family, she had 3 other siblings, one sister and two brothers. Amelia's father was a daily wage laborer who earned handsome amount of money on daily bases and her mother never went to school. The couple was very much fond of each other's company. In spite of their problems they both respected and cared for each other.

They were somehow managing their day to day needs, so when Amelia's mother came to know that she is pregnant for the 4th time with Amelia, the couple decided that this time they don't want the baby as they already had other kids. Amelia's parents were already facing tough time handling the whole family and this new baby will be more of added burden towards them.

So the next morning they decided to go for an abortion, as they were waiting in the clinic for their turn to come. Many feelings were running down their mind. *Is this the right decision we are making to abort a child?* Amelia's mother whispered slowly, realizing that even her father acknowledged that he was feeling the same. They had never done this before with their other kids. On the other hand, they were also contemplating how they would cope with the new baby's needs, as they were already living hand to mouth.

After some moments they both started to pray, "Oh Almighty, please guide us and let us take that action which is better in our favor," as they were just saying the prayer in heart. It was their time to go in, as the mother laid on the bed and father waited outside. The doctor came in and started to check her and the baby. It showed the heartbeat of the baby. Hearing this, tears rolled down her eyes, and she felt a sudden sense of distress. She told the doctor, "I don't want to proceed with the abortion. Please stop the process." She went out crying, and the father, seeing her, rushed to ask her what had happened then she said I have heard our baby's heartbeat, just now it's breaking me to take this step, so I have decided to not do the abortion. I am not feeling right to do it. Whatever will happen, we will see. Again the father asked, *"Is this your last thought?"*

Thinking about their circumstances, she said, "Yes, it is and I am not going back in."

And they came back home. Day by day it became more difficult for them to survive with just the father earning daily wage. Some days the father would starve himself but feed the kids and mother as she was pregnant. If they would not have enough food, they would often not sleep thinking what would happen in the near future. How will things go? How will we manage?

Months passed by and it was the day when Amelia was going to be born. The mother packed her small bag to take along with her to city's Charity Hospital. In the car both the mother and the father were worried for safe arrival of the new born and the mother's safety. They were nervous as she was taken in the O.T. The father waited patiently outside along with other kids. At around 10:10 am Amelia was born. She was super cute and beautiful. The nurse handed the baby to the father. He saw her and cried, cried and cried. Holding her he felt so much of peace and joy. He went to see his wife and to show her the baby. Holding the baby the couple cried together saying one another how can we once thought about taking the life of this precious little angel. They were both happy with their decision of keeping the baby, both the mother and the baby were healthy.

The father initiated the process of discharge, so the mother and the baby got discharge from the hospital. That same night a man was passing by in his car, all of sudden his car broke down and stopped working in the middle of the road. He tried many time to get it started but all in vain. He saw here and there, no one was there, then he came near the small house where Amelia's parents live. He knocked slowly on the door. Amelia's father opened the door to see who is there at this hour of night while holding a knife in the other hand to check on with the stranger. He saw there was a man standing. The father asked, "Who are you and what do you want?"

The man at the door said, "I am sorry to disturb you at this hour of night." He explained that his car broke down and there is no one around here other than this house, so I have come here to ask for help. "I am hungry."

The father said, "I am a poor man and just about a while back I bought my new born and wife home as she had given birth today. I will see around the house if I find any food which I can offer you." He told the man to come in and sit. The man sat there, occasionally hearing the cries of the newborn baby. The other kids were sleeping. The father went to check for food in the fridge. It was empty. He saw in the cupboard there was nothing as well. Just as he was about to close the cabinet, he saw little flour in it. He immediately kneaded a dough and made bread out of it. He came out and gave the bread to the man to eat. The father said, "I am sorry I have checked all my house but there was only flour with which I have prepared the bread for u. Please, accept it."

The man happily accepted it as he was hungry. He ate the bread and was about to go but the father said to the man, "It's very late. You can rest here if you want and go the next day." The man accepted it.

It was next day morning he left after greeting the father and thanking him for his hospitality and generosity. The same evening the same man came carrying loads of food, groceries and clothes for the family. He said to the father, "Please accept the things from me." With that he started to share what had happen. "I am a business man. I travel city to city for my business and yesterday night when my car broke down at the middle of the road I was in different city so could not even call my family or friend for help as it was late night, so after waiting for about some hours alone I walked for some time and saw a small house which was yours. When you opened the door and tried to help me out by making me the bread in spite of you going through hunger and just had a baby, the same moment I thought I wanted to do something good for you. I am offering you a job in one of my company here. You can join in from tomorrow." The father thanked the man for it and said him, "This is the blessing which came our way through my daughter, Amelia." And he cried again.

The man offered the father with his dream job and gave him salary which was beyond his expectation. Things started to get better for the family.

The kids were going to good school. They bought a new house. After a while a new car and so on. Their lives just started to get better and better.

From very young age Amelia was a very intelligent girl, she would often get good grades. She was also loved by many people around her for her kindness. She would always help anyone who was in need. She was strong and courageous.

With time she become one of the beautiful women in town. Everyone who passed by her always use to adore her beauty but she would not care much of it. She would only care for her family.

The man who offered Amelia's father with job passed away on a flight crash. From then started new turn for Amelia and her parents.

Amelia's sibling never cared or respected their parents, only Amelia would take care for them. Amelia's two brothers and one sister got married and shifted to other countries with their respective families. They would not even bother to send them money or anything for months. They were only happy with their new own family.

As with time Amelia's father grown old and her mother's eyesight become weak. None from the sibling would come to visit them. Amelia would always be available for them, taking care of them.

One morning Amelia's father woke up with sharp pain in his chest. He was screaming with the pain keeping his hand on the chest. He called Amelia, "Oh, Amelia, come fast." Amelia heard it and rushed towards him. She asked him, "What happened, Father?"

He said, "It's an unbearable pain I am feeling on my chest."

She said, "Father, let's go to hospital." She immediately took his father on the wheel chair towards her car. Inside the car she would keep calming her father as his cries increased with that he got unconscious. Amelia shouted, "Father, Father, Father." With tears rolling down her eyes. In the hospital she rushed to the reception and told them about her father's condition. The officer at the reception took all the details and said to wait. Meanwhile he called the hospital's staff to bring the roller bed. The staff carried her father and placed him on the bed. They immediately admitted him.

As Amelia was waiting for doctor's word, she went to a small prayer hall inside the hospital and started to pray, "Oh, Almighty, please help my father. Please cure him. Please save him. Ohh, Almighty, I don't want to lose him please." She started crying profusely.

Her mother was in home due to her eyesight problem. Amelia spoke to her mother on phone and told her not to worry about her father. She said he will be fine as she did not want her mother to take stress out of it as even her mother was going through eyesight problem. As she was on phone the doctor came. She told her mother to take rest and she will take care of everything.

Amelia rushed to doctor and asked about her father's condition. The doctor paused for a while and said your father had a mild heart attack this morning and we have to keep him in observation for some days here so they had shifted the father in critical heart care ward. Hearing this Amelia could not bear it and again started crying. The doctor calmed her down and said he will be fine just pray for him.

On the other hand, Amelia contacted his siblings to say about their father's condition. One brother said I am in other country for my business meeting and the other one said I am on holiday with my family. In spite being in same city no one came. Her sister was also in other country with his husband's family so even she did not make it.

After 12 hours her father regained consciousness. The doctor called Amelia in his cabin and said her about it but with that he said still he is in critical mode, we need some more days to shift him to general ward.

Amelia was running between hospital to home and home to hospital, as she was only the one caring for both ailing parents. She was also worried for money as whatever they had saved earlier had finished, as her father was already a BP patient and mother had weak eyesight so for their medicines, food, hospital visit money finished. Her brothers would not send them any money so nothing was left with them.

Amelia would often pray for her ailing parents and also she would pray how will I cover the cost of the hospital. What's going to happen? On the other hand she was happy that at least her father had regained consciousness. Her mother said her in home to take her to see her father in hospital. Amelia said I will take you once he is shifted to general ward. After two days they shifted the father to general ward. He was fine again. She was happy for him and thanked Almighty for it. As her mother would say, "Take me to visit your father in the hospital." So, she took her mother, as promised, to see his father. The mother went to check on her father, and they spent some time together alone. During that time, they expressed to each other, "See, this girl, Amelia, whom we once thought of not bringing into this world and considered aborting, is the same girl standing with us in our toughest phase." They both cried as they shared these sentiments, acknowledging that their other kids didn't even bother to look for them.

Amelia went to the same prayer hall in the hospital and started to thank the Almighty for his father's health improvement and also she started praying for the money to pay for his father's medical bill. She said, "Ohh Almighty, thank you so much for my father's health. Please, ohh Almighty, make a way for me to pay my father's bill as well. I am in dire need of money at this moment." She began crying loudly, saying it as there was no one who was in the prayer hall. Then a women heard her saying all this while entering the prayer hall. She greeted Amelia and said, "What happened to you? Why are you crying so loudly?"

Amelia just nodded her head and said, "It's nothing, it's nothing."

Then the women asked again to her, "What happened? Just say to me."

As Amelia started to talk, she shared everything from her father's hospitalization to his health improvement. She said, "I have no money with me. How can I pay for him? My brothers are there but they don't bother to even come and see my ailing father. They don't give any money for his treatment either. Even my mother is having health issues due to her weak eyesight."

Hearing this the unknown lady said, "It is fine, my child, you don't need to worry about your bill. It will be paid from my side to you."

Amelia said to her, "Please don't joke with me like this. I am already going through enough." She thought maybe she is just saying that to make me calm down.

As she could not believe it, the lady again said, "Trust me, I will bare all the cost of your father's treatment." Hearing it again built trust in Amelia. At the very moment Amelia bowed down to the ground and thank the Almighty for this glad news that the help came from this unknown lady. She also thanked the lady for this great help.

She said, "Thank you, madam, for the help you have given to me."

Amelia was happy and relieved. She went to see her father. Her father was asleep. Amelia told the nurse to give some food to her father. The nurse said it is coming in a while. Amelia waited for a while, then the food came. Amelia slowly woke her father up.

"Oh, Father, get up, Father. Your food has come." Her father woke up and sat on the bed. Amelia started to feed her father with her hand. She saw in the food tray there was a small bread, a soup, yogurt, boiled vegetable, a small fish which was also boiled. She asked her father what will he eat first. His father nodded head and said, "Feed me the soup first." She began feeding him the soup and rest of the food. Her father drank only the soup and had yogurt but he said, "I don't feel to eat the vegetable and the fish."

Amelia said, "Father, eat everything, you need to recover fast, Father. If you don't eat, the medicine will not work on you." Then somehow her father ate the vegetable and fish. As everything was done, Amelia said, "Father, now you take rest. I will just go home and drop mother, will take a short nap and come back." All this while, her mother was on the side bed where her father was. As she was leaving, her father said, "Okay, my lovely daughter, you can go home." As she departed, her father kissed her hand, expressing his gratitude, "Thank you so much for everything you have done for me thus far."

Amelia said to him, "Why do you thank me? I am doing my duty towards you. You are my father and I am blessed to have you as my father." That bought a broad smile on her father's face, also a feeling of guilt was also going on and off with him that they don't wanted this child to be born once but the parents never shared this with Amelia that they did not wanted her in this world.

Amelia said, "Don't worry, Father, about anything. I will be back soon to you." Amelia left with her mother for home. Upon reaching, she took a shower and then prepared a meal with some vegetables and bread, which they both ate. Afterward, they went to sleep. During her sleep, she received a call from the hospital. The nurse was on the other line, urgently requesting her to rush to the hospital as it was an emergency.

Amelia's mother was fast asleep so she don't woke her and ran towards her car. On the way she had different feelings. She said, "What if something happen to Father?" But then she said her father was fine while she was leaving for home. She reached hospital. There she rushed towards the nurse who spoke to her on phone. The nurse gave Amelia devastating news about her father. She said, "Your father had two big heart attack all of sudden in span of 1hr and he is no more." Amelia started crying loudly. Hearing it she ran to see her father, she then kissed him on head with all feelings running on her mind, *but why did I leave him and go? Why was not I with him when he left? How this happen all of sudden? He was fine when I left.* The nurse started to calm Amelia down saying, "It is all God's will. We can't do anything other than praying for him now." After a while, Amelia calmed down, and she said to herself, "What shall I say, Mother? How will I break the news to her about Father's passing?" She then started to phone her brothers. With a trembling voice, she informed both of her brothers, "Brother, Brother, our father has passed away." Upon hearing this, the brothers did not express much emotion. They nonchalantly responded, "He left? Oh, okay, that's fine." They further mentioned, "We are busy with our work, so we can't make it for the funeral," and promptly ended the call. Amelia started to cry more and more, "Why you took my father away? Ohh Almighty, why are my brothers of no help? Why? Why? Why? It's me again."

As she was saying all these, the unknown lady who met her in the prayer hall was passing and she saw Amelia crying she came to her and asked, "What's wrong, my child? Is everything okay with you?"

Amelia said, "My most precious thing, my father, has passed away and during that moment I was not with him. I am feeling guilty about it. Why did I leave him and go home? Why this happened? Why was I not with him in his last moments?"

The women calmed Amelia down and said, "Listen my child, we can't change what just happen and now your father just needs prayers. Also you need to be strong now for your mother." After a while Amelia gathered all the courage. She than told the hospital authorities to prepare for her father's discharge, as she said this to hospital authorities. The lady who was with her said to Amelia, "You go home now and get your mother ready for the funeral while I will take care of your father's bill." Meanwhile Amelia went to home as she wanted to say the news of her father's passing to her mother while being with her as she was also ailing patient, so she did not wanted her mother to feel the pain all alone. On the way she stopped the car and started to clean her face as to see that she wasn't crying to her mother. She went in home where she saw her mother resting on her roller chair. Amelia came in and her mother started to ask her, "What happen, dear? Why did you left home so early in morning?" Amelia at first did not said anything but then she came near her mother, kept her hand on her mother's shoulder. There she said,

"Mother, please don't lose your patience. I am about to say you a news."

"Ohh, my mother, father has passed away." And she began to hug her mother tightly. They both cried for some time and then Amelia said, "Let's go, Mother, we have to go to hospital and get father's body for his last rites." So they went to pick her father's body. There they took the body in the ambulance while her mother was crying badly. Amelia was just comforting her, while on funeral none of her brother's came nor her sister, so she and her mother were the only one. After some days Amelia's mother asked her, "How did you manage to pay the bill of your father? We had nothing with us then."

That time Amelia said, "Ohh all this while I totally forgotten about the kind full unknown lady who helped pay father's bill in hospital."

Her mother said, "We need to go to her house and thank her for everything." The next day Amelia and her mother went to the unknown lady's house. As Amelia knocked on the door, the unknown lady opened the door and greeted Amelia and her mother.

"Welcome, welcome," she said. "It's you, my child, come inside, have a sit." The lady served them some cookies and coffee. The lady asked Amelia, "How are you now? How is everything going with you?"

Amelia said, "It is not easy losing my father but we have just started to cope with the passing away of my father," Amelia said. "We will never forget him but we have to cope somehow." Amelia's mother started to speak to the lady and thanked her for the help she has given for paying the hospital bill.

The lady then started, "No, no, it's nothing what I did. Actually when I saw Amelia for the first time in the prayer hall I was stuck as I have also lost my only girl who is of same age as Amelia in an accident 6 months back. Amelia relate with her so much so whenever I see Amelia in her I see my daughter in her and she started to weep."

Amelia said, "I am your daughter, why are you crying, ohh, my mother?" Hearing her say those words to the lady, the lady and Amelia both hugged each other. Amelia whispered, "I have got two mothers now, who care for me, that's so great to have you both as my mother." With a broad smile on her face, the lady then hand over an envelope with money inside to Amelia. Amelia said, "No need of it. We will manage. You have already helped us enough."

The lady said, "As you have called me your mother now, you have to keep this money for your needs and also, my child, I am always available for you if you ever need me." Then Amelia and her mother left.

After some months, Amelia's mother health Detroit more and she also passed away, so now only Amelia was alone in home. Her brother or sister never cared for her or the parents. They never bother to even take Amelia's call now. As stated earlier Amelia was a very bright, talented, beautiful, young lady but she was all occupied in between her ailing parents' need as no one was there to care for them, so that's why she did not even worked before, so somehow she gather herself up and told herself in the mirror, "It's your time now, Amelia. Stand up, Amelia, stand up for yourself, Amelia." So she started to groom herself up daily. She started to take yoga classes. She ate healthy food. She also starting searching jobs for herself meanwhile she on and off visited that lady as now she was like her mother. Amelia got a job in a very good multinational company. There she prospered and got promoted within span of 1yr. She also took driving license. She also use to do many charity works. Whenever she saw someone in need, she would help them. She started a charity school for the under privileged kids. She educated them by herself after she would come back from her work. She also use to feed stray cats and dog around her home daily, gradually she started her business of skin care and cosmetic brand. Her brand in few year was one of the top brands in town. She was a successful person just by herself. For every small achievements she would thank Almighty first, then she would feed some laborers around to feel the blessings she had. She was famous by now.

One fine morning she went to visit her other mother as she use to regularly go and visit her, as her other mother was getting old. There she saw her on the floor slipped in the bathroom and become unconscious. Amelia rushed towards her and shook her up mother, mother get up. She called the ambulance and she took her to the hospital. She waited for the doctor there. The doctor came and said, "Your mother has a fracture in her legs due to the fall."

Earlier many times Amelia had said to her other mother, "Come and stay with me. Why you live alone here?" But she would not listen then but now she said,

"Mother, please come and stay with me. You have a leg fracture. I will take care of you."

She insisted and said, "Am I not your daughter? Please come with me to home." She took her other mother to her home and took good care of her by herself. She would prepare food for her. She would bathed her up. She would dress her. She would make her bed. She even use to take her on wheel chair for fresh air outside in park, as days went by the lady's fractured leg got healed completely the lady was recovered. The lady said, "Let me go to my house; it's been days since I've been there," Amelia said. "Oh, Mother, why don't you come here completely and stay with me? I am alone here. Why do you have to live alone in that house?" After insisting for some time, the lady said to Amelia, "Just take me home, and we will come back." The lady went home, took some of her belongings along with a photo of her daughter, and came to stay with Amelia. From that point on, the lady and Amelia lived together. Amelia hired a house help and an assistant for them.

Things were going great with Amelia she was known among the people as lady with heart of Gold. As some days went by, Amelia receive a call from a lady. With her was another lady on the call. The ladies spoke, "Hello, is this Amelia?"

Amelia said, "Yes, it is, who is it?"

She said, "We both are your brother's wife (different)."

Amelia said, "Yes. Tell me what happen? You called me after so many years. Is everything okay?"

Even though her brothers never cared then, also Amelia use to care for them that made Amelia as a pure soul good with heart. The lady said, "We are calling you to say that it's been years. Your brothers don't have any work and our children don't live with us. They have shifted with their families to other countries. They neglected us completely. They don't take our calls. Even your other brother don't have work and he has started to have insomnia from past some years. Due to taking all the stress your both brothers never wanted us to contact you as they felt guilty for everything they have done to you and their parents. Every day they bowed down to the ground and cry and ask for forgiveness for what they have done for past those years. They missed their parents now but we don't have anything left in our house. We sleep on empty stomach and also we can't see our husband like this that's why we are calling you secretly."

Amelia said, "Just tell me where you live, I am coming in a while to you."

It was late in the night Amelia called her driver and went with him to fetch some groceries along with basic needs things. She came to the address that her brother's wives gave. It was a small hut. Seeing it she became sad that her brother were going through a lot. She then rang the bell. At first her brother did not recognize her. He opened the door and asked, "Who are you? What led you here at this hour lady?"

Amelia said. "You forgot me? Won't you call your little sister inside? I am Amelia."

His brother bowed down to her crying, "Ohh, Amelia, ohh, Amelia, ohh, Amelia, please forgive me for everything we have done to you. I can't ask forgiveness from our parents as they are not with us but I can ask you to forgive me."

Amelia told to her brother, "Get up." and then hugged him tightly. They both started crying as it was years Amelia and her brother did not met, then Amelia's brother told her to come inside his home and sit. Amelia said to driver, "Please get all the groceries in." The house was filled with loads of groceries, then came his other brother from a nearby house.

He saw a car and whispered, "Who is this lady came at this hour of night? Whose car is it? Let me check."

So he went inside. There he saw his other brother crying with the lady, this brother also did not recognized Amelia so he asked, "Who are you?"

Then Amelia said, "Even you have forgotten me. I am Amelia, your sister." And they also hugged and cried as well. Then they called their sister who was in other country with her husband and his family. She also came to them and then it was a great reunion. They also bowed down and thanked Almighty for this unforgettable reunion of siblings.

Amelia said to her siblings, "You can't change what you did with me and our parents. It should not have happen on first place. See now what you have done with our parents. Your children are doing same with you. What you sow will reap someday, somehow. It's just how Almighty work but now you feel guilty and you ask for forgiveness, that's good and Almighty loves whoever ask for forgiveness and HE also forgives just start your fresh life again with goodness in your heart for everyone."

Amelia told his brothers to shift to her house with their wives as now Amelia had a big and beautiful house. Her brothers along with their wife shifted to her house. After much insisting, there they met that lady. Amelia introduced them to each other. She said, "Mother, they are my brothers." To her, brothers and sister she said, "This is my mother, who helped me in paying our fathers hospitalization bills and she does not have anyone so I am the one taking care of her now as she is old." Both the brother thanked her and the whole family started to care and respect the lady like their own mother. Amelia gave in charge of her two offices to her two brothers and told them to join in the business. The brother again started to work, everything in the house was going great again. Everyone was happy, everyone was smiling and the brothers said to Amelia, "You have made us so proud, we are so much blessed to have a sister like you by our side!"

As Amelia use to feed stray cats and dog, one day a man passing in his car saw Amelia doing it. He was amazed by the sight of it, then he kept on coming at the same time and see Amelia feeding the cats daily from distance. He would see her feed and say lovely words to them. He started to have many feelings towards her. He wanted to meet her somehow. He gathered the courage and went to her and said, "I see you daily here and I felt in love with your first glance. May I ask you for your hand in marriage?" That man did not know anything about Amelia. Even Amelia did not know anything of him but after seeing the guy even Amelia started to have feelings at their first glance.

Amelia said, "If you want to marry me you can bring proposal to my house. I have my mother and brothers who will decide for it." The man did not waited and next day he came to Amelia's home with his parents. He knocked on the door. Amelia's brother opened it and told them to come in and sit. They said, "We have come with proposal for your sister Amelia and we wanted them to marry as soon as possible." By then Amelia was Age 42.

The brother told, "Let me ask my sister and reply you for it." Then they left. Amelia's brother came to her and said, "Sister, they bought a proposal for you. Are you willing to marry this guy?"

As Amelia had already seen the guy, she said, "YES, I am okay to marry him."

The wedding preparation began gradually and Amelia got married to this guy. The first evening of their wedding night, they both bowed down to ground and thanked Almighty along with praying for their new journey together, then the guy kissed on Amelia's head and said to her, "I had always dreamed of marrying someone like you and Almighty has blessed me the women of my dreams." The guy was the sweetest man a women can have as a husband. He would care for every little thing which Amelia wanted and also use to keep her happy. Amelia felt blessed about it too. After 2 years, at the age of 44 years, Amelia gave birth to their triplet's babies, two girls and one boy. Amelia's kid grew to be very respectful kids and they all lived happily. Amelia started doing more social and charitable work her husband use to support her for it too.

After some years Amelia passed away peacefully during her sleep. Everyone who knew Amelia came to her funeral and cried profusely as she had helped many, many people around, even the cats and dog who she fed daily came to her funeral. They sat next to her body, silent, tears were rolling down from their eyes too.

Amelia's children later on built charitable hospital on their mother's name called AMELIA, which gives free treatment for all those who can't afford.

www.ingramcontent.com/pod-product-compliance
Lightning Source LLC
Chambersburg PA
CBHW022012170726
47994CB00026B/3165